KV-511-032

This book belongs to:

_____

A catalogue record for this book is available from the British Library

Published by Ladybird Books Ltd
80 Strand, London, WC2R 0RL
A Penguin Company

2 4 6 8 10 9 7 5 3 1
© LADYBIRD BOOKS LTD MMIX
LADYBIRD and the device of a Ladybird are trademarks of Ladybird Books Ltd

ISBN: 978-140930-172-1

Printed in China

Five-minute Tales
Fastest Pony Ever

written by Marie Birkinshaw
illustrated by Caroline Freake

Speedy Goes Shopping

Speedy the pony loves galloping as fast
as she can. That's how she got her name
– Speedy, the fastest little pony ever.
In her hurry, Speedy often gets things
wrong or gets in the way. But Farmer
Henry doesn't mind. He knows
that Speedy is only trying to help.

One spring day, Farmer Henry was very busy with the lambs. "This is hot work, Speedy," he said. He wiped his eyes and mopped his head.

Speedy galloped away. She filled a bucket full of water for Farmer Henry. Zoom! Back she came. But most of the water had spilled!

"Thank you, Speedy," said Farmer Henry, kindly. "I'm sorry, but I don't have an apple for you today and I don't have time to go shopping. Perhaps you can help?" Farmer Henry gave Speedy a shopping list. Speedy didn't waste a second. She galloped to fetch her mum, Honey.

First they went to the bakery. Speedy showed the baker the list. The baker helped to fill up their bags.

carrot cake

Next, the two ponies visited the dairy. While Honey looked for yoghurts and cheese, Speedy decided to speed things up by choosing some eggs. Whoops!

Last of all, the ponies bought some apples. The shopping was all done. Speedy galloped home, in a hurry!

Farmer Henry patted Honey's mane
and handed an apple to Speedy.
"Well done, Speedy," he said. "That's the
fastest shopping ever!"

Speedy to the Rescue

It was a hot summer's day. Farmer Henry was working hard, and Speedy was racing around, doing her best to help. The farmer's two children, Tom and Lucy, came to see them. They were pulling their go-karts.

"We're going to meet some friends to have a race," said Lucy.
"Why don't you go along too, Speedy?" said Farmer Henry. Speedy was so excited that she galloped all around the field!

Three… two… one… the go-karts set off down the hill. Lucy took the lead, but she was soon overtaken by her friend Jamie. Tom caught the edge of the kerb and came to a stop. Crunch! Luckily, no one was hurt.

But where was Speedy? Right at the front of course! Fast little ponies love races. But suddenly – ker-ching! Jamie lost control and headed straight for the pond… going faster and faster! "Speedy to the rescue," neighed the fastest little pony.

Speedy galloped down the hill faster
and faster.
"Help!" Jamie shouted.
Speedy galloped as quickly as she
could after him.

The go-kart turned off the path. But just as Jamie hit the water, Speedy put on a final burst of speed and overtook him.

Speedy pushed Jamie's go-kart to one side away from the water.
But she couldn't stop herself in time and Speedy landed in the water with a great big SPLASH!

"Three cheers for Speedy," shouted the children. "HIP, HIP, HOORAY!" "You're the fastest and the wettest pony ever," laughed Tom and Lucy. Speedy gave them a cheeky smile. Then she shook the water out of her mane, and gave everyone a soaking.

Speedy Wins the Race

It was the day of the village show. Farmer Henry only had a few more jobs to do before he was ready to set off. Speedy had been racing about helping him all morning.

Finally, they got to the stables. Speedy picked up brushes, combs and ribbons and took them to Farmer Henry. He was getting her mum, Honey, ready for the prettiest pony competition.
He led Honey out to the truck.

After so much helping and running around, Speedy suddenly felt very tired. She snuggled down in the straw of the stable and fell asleep. Meanwhile, Farmer Henry finished loading up the truck.

"Ponies… sheep… vegetables…
Yes, everything's ready," said Farmer Henry.
He closed the truck door and put on his
seat belt. Brrrm! He started up the engine
and set off.

The sound of the engine woke Speedy.
She ran out into the yard and saw
Farmer Henry's truck heading away
down the road.

"Wait for me!" she neighed. But Farmer
Henry couldn't hear her. Speedy galloped
after the truck. She took a short cut across
the field and jumped over the stream.

She carried on galloping as fast as she could. Soon, she reached the showground. The sound of loud cheers and clapping made her run even faster.

BANG! A race was just starting. But Speedy didn't notice. The little pony just galloped faster and faster…

She didn't stop galloping… until she reached the finish line! Honey and Farmer Henry rushed over to meet her.

"There you are, Speedy!" said Farmer Henry.

What a day! Honey had won the prettiest pony prize, and Farmer Henry's vegetables were some of the biggest and best.
And of course, Speedy had won the race!
"Well done, Speedy," said Farmer Henry.
"You really are the fastest little pony ever!"